CW00855012

Write to: Hunt & Thorpe, Laurel House, Station Approach,
New Alresford, Hampshire SO24 9JH, UK

Hunt & Thorpe is a name used under licence by Paternoster Publishing,
PO Box 300, Kingstown Broadway, Carlisle, CA3 0QW

For Douglas, Fiona and Katie Learmond

A CIP catalogue record for this book is available from the British Library

Manufactured in Hong Kong

The Angel who flew backwards to Christmas

Written by **Liz Joy**
Illustrated by **Carolyn Dinan**

HUNT & THORPE

baternoster
publishing

strid was an angel with a difference. She was not like the ones you see in church windows. Astrid had short, dark hair and a halo that slipped sideways. She was always late and mostly it did not matter, but today it did. Today was the day that the angels in Astrid's group were to be given their full set of wings. They woke early and excited. Then they went to a special cloud, which was pink and soft with the glitter of candyfloss.

So dazzling was the light all about them that Astrid thought she had lost her halo, outshone as it was by the brilliance. She went off to look for it and lost her way. By the time she returned, there was no sign of her friends.

"Where is everybody?" She wondered aloud. Then she saw
something lying a little way off. When she reached it, Astrid
discovered to her delight that it was a full set of wings.   "I
suppose a full set of wings would feel strange at first," she
muttered as she struggled to put them on, "but they are
lovely." She gave the wings a little flap and to her surprise
she was moving through the air, not forwards but ...

BACKWARDS! "Oh dear!" said Astrid, "this can't be
right. Wherever will I end up?" But there was nobody there
to tell her. She wanted to look for the other angels but she
had no control over her wings at all. They flapped of their
own accord and Astrid flew faster and faster. She was not
just going BACKWARDS but DOWNWARDS as well.

Astrid felt almost afraid, but then she saw a huge, beautiful ball floating in space. She recognised the patterns on it from her lessons in the angels' schoolroom.

"This must be Earth!" exclaimed Astrid. "That is why we were practising our alleluias. Something very special is going to happen there." And although she felt the huge ball pulling her towards it, she began to feel braver and even excited as she rushed down to Earth. With the help of her wings she even managed to land the right way up.

A little way off she saw a light flickering on the ground like
a distant star. It was a camp fire and sitting round it were
three kings. Astrid knew at once that they were kings
because they were all wearing crowns. She felt very shy as
she approached them, even though at home in the heavens
above she was known for her bouncy friendliness. The
three kings turned to look at their unexpected visitor.

"Look, we have company," the first king said. "You are most welcome," said the second king, bowing to Astrid.

"Delighted to see you," said the third king, who was the youngest and most relaxed. "What lovely wings you have."

"They are my new ones," Astrid replied to the third king, "but to tell you the truth, they're not very easy to manage and now I am awfully late. But I can't remember what it is I am late for or where I am meant to be going, and I've lost the rest of my friends.

"Pray, do not worry little angel," said the second king kindly. "Let us help you."

The first king, who was the eldest and thought that he should take charge, said: "Certainly we can shed some light on the matter for you." But he stopped, suddenly feeling rather foolish, as shedding light was something that angels did all the time. There was indeed a gentle glow of light all around Astrid. She smiled at the first king and he continued:

"See that star up there." Astrid looked and saw that one star among the thousands of others twinkling above was bigger, and shone more brightly, than all the rest.

The second king continued: "We saw it rise and have followed it from the East. We believe it is leading us to Bethlehem, where we shall find a baby King has been born."

"A baby!" cried Astrid, her wings flapping enthusiastically. "Of course! They were lighting up that special comet only the other day." The heavenly bells that had been ringing faintly in her memory jangled into tune and she remembered everything.

"That's right! God the heavenly father is sending down his son to live on Earth. The alleluias we've been practising are to welcome him. How could I have forgotten?"

Astrid began to get into a flap. Her wings worked faster and faster as she flew around backwards in ever widening circles. The third king tried to catch up with her. "Little angel," he called. "I think I know what is wrong with your wings. Wait a moment please!" But the little angel's wings carried her further away and all she could do was wave goodbye. "Godspeed!" her three new friends called after her.

As he saw the little angel's light fade away in the distance, the third king felt sad, as though he had lost something precious.

Astrid's wings flew her backwards very fast, chasing the comet's kindly light. Beneath her on the hillside she saw sheep that looked like tiny clouds, but she could not see where she was going.   CRASH!

Astrid found herself entangled in a tree that was sticking up, unexpectedly, on the top of a hill. Try as she might, she could not get free.

She began to sing alleluias to keep herself cheerful, although, deep in her heart, she knew that God the heavenly father would be watching over her. Sheep came hurrying from all over the hillside to investigate the strange noise in the tree.

"Don't worry, sheep," called the leader of the flock. "It's only one of those angels that have been around the place recently."

"My name is Astrid," said the little angel to the leader of the sheep, with as much dignity as she could muster. "Did I hear you mention angels? I am trying to find the rest of my friends."

"Ah yes, so sorry," said the leader, looking sheepish. He had forgotten that the little angel would be able to understand him.

"My name is Sim. Can we do anything to help get you down?" "Yes please!" Astrid said gratefully. "I'm in a great hurry to get to Bethlehem."

"That's just over the hill," said Sim. The sheep all began to baa and shake the tree. Astrid's wings beat at the branches and suddenly she landed with her feet on the ground.

"I'm glad that worked," said Sim. "If your wings are giving you trouble, why don't we walk to Bethlehem? Angels can walk as well as fly, can't they?"

"Of course they can," said Astrid and they set off down the hill together.

"We've never seen angels before," said Sim. "They were so bright that it was like the sun coming out in the middle of the night. They sang beautifully."

"Angelically," said Astrid. "But we have been practising awfully hard. Do you know where the baby is?"

"Yes. Jesus is in a stable with the animals. Our shepherds have gone to see him. Mary and Joseph, his earthly parents, couldn't find anywhere else to stay."

"It's just the sort of thing God would want to do, to include the animals in something as special as this," said Astrid.

"You see the bright light over there?" asked Sim. "That's where the angels are singing round the stable." As he spoke, the air was filled with the crystal clear sound of alleluias.

Astrid's wings began to flap with excitement. Then it came to her in a flash.

"Sim!" she shouted. "I know what's wrong with my wings. I've put them on BACK TO FRONT! No wonder I could only fly BACKWARDS!"

The angels heard Astrid's shout and they flew over to greet
her with great rapture.

"Astrid! It's good to see you safe
and sound," said the angel teacher.
"We were just going to send out a
search party for you. Now let's get
your wings on the right way round.
It's a wonder you made it here at all."
"Sim and the sheep helped me,"
said Astrid, as they were led into the stable.

Astrid thought there was something wonderful about the little baby asleep in the hay; with Mary and Joseph and the animals watching him peacefully.

Then the three kings arrived with their presents, and they were very pleased to meet their little angel again. The third king, watching Astrid's delight as she hovered over the baby Jesus, thought happily: "None of us need ever again feel that we have lost something precious."

The three kings, speaking together, said: "Whether we are young or old, wise or foolish or, like the little angel, in so much of a muddle that we fly backwards to Christmas; it really doesn't matter, just so long as we get there in ..."

The End